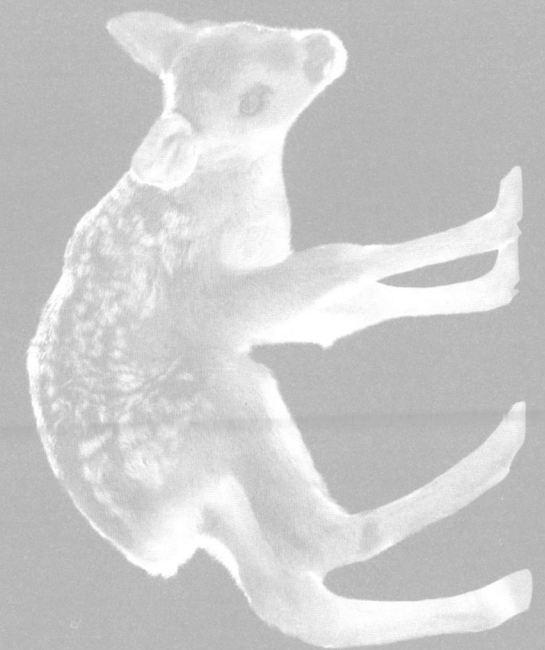

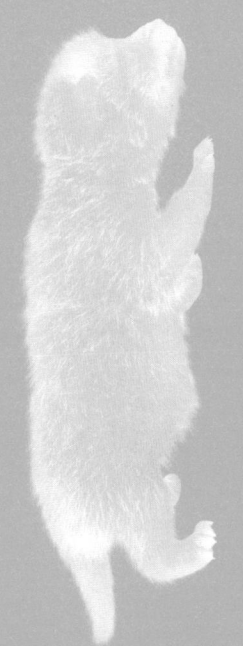

See how they grow
Forest

DK

Mouse pup

I have just been born into
a cozy underground nest.
My mother has come
to feed me milk.
I am very hungry!

I have no fur and I cannot see or hear.
My hair starts to grow after a few days
but my eyes and ears are still closed.

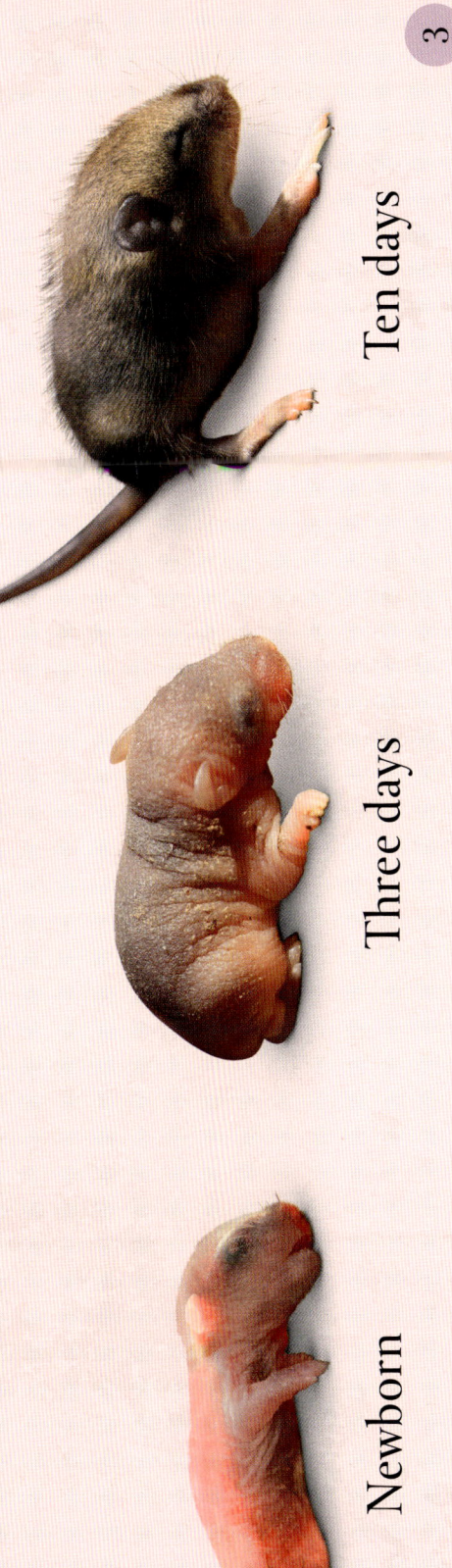

Ten days

Three days

Newborn

My eyes are finally open, and my claws are becoming sharp. As my legs get stronger, I take my first steps and start to explore.

Two weeks

Four weeks

Now I am almost as big as my mother. I can find my own food, and my long tail helps me to balance as I scurry around.

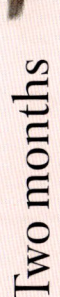

Two months

Squirrel kit

I am a newborn squirrel kit
with my brothers and sisters
in a treetop nest. I have no
hair and I cannot see.

My fur starts to grow after a few days.
I am still very sleepy and I stay safe in my warm, dry home.

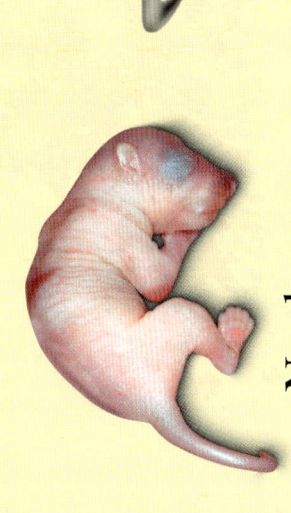

Newborn

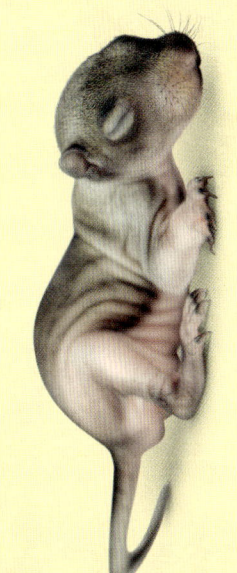

Two weeks

Three weeks

My eyes have opened and my legs are getting stronger. I can now leave the nest and start to explore the treetops—but I never go far from home.

Four weeks

Six weeks

I love to eat nuts! I find them by searching in trees and on the forest floor. Soon, I will be as big as my mother.

Mother squirrel

Ten weeks

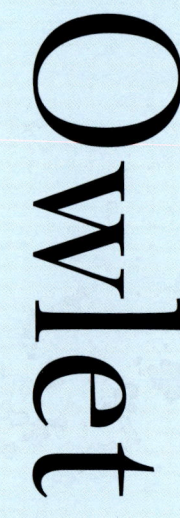

Owlet

I am an owlet growing
inside one of the eggs
that my mother has laid.
She is keeping me warm
until I'm ready to hatch.

Peck, peck, peck! I chip away at the egg until I am out. My fluffy down feathers begin to grow but my eyes are still closed.

Five days

Newborn

Hatching

Now I can see, walk, and jump! My wing feathers are growing through my fluffy white down.

Ten days

Three weeks

Five weeks

As my wings get stronger, I practice flying and prepare to leave the nest. I can glide through the air and hunt for my own food.

Three months

Seven weeks

Fox cub

I am a newborn cub. I can't see or hear, but I can smell my brother and sister nearby. My mother keeps us safe.

My eyes are now open and I can start to explore the world outside our den. I'm getting bigger every day and my fur is growing thicker.

Newborn

Two weeks

Four weeks

My legs and paws grow stronger.
I can now hear the smallest sounds
and sniff many new smells.

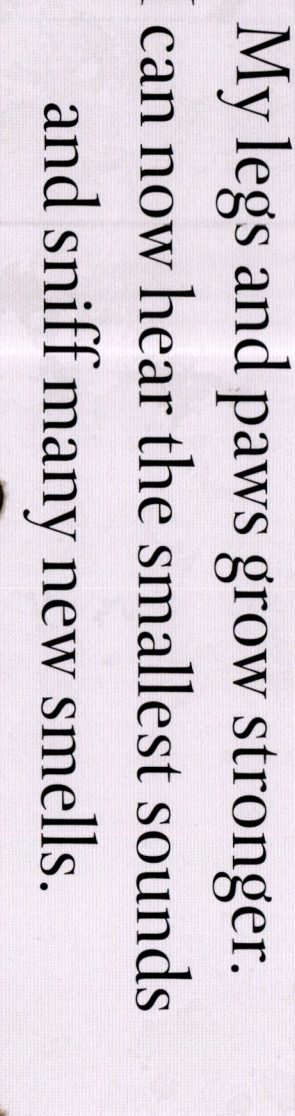

Six weeks

Eight weeks

Ten
weeks

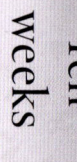

I have a long, bushy tail and a thick red coat of fur. I am a good hunter and can find my own food.

Twelve weeks

Fawn

I am a newborn fawn.
My mother looks after me
and hides me in the long
grass to keep me safe.

My fur is speckled with white spots.
It helps me hide in the forest.
My mother helps me get on my feet
and feeds me to make me strong.

Two weeks

A few days

Six weeks

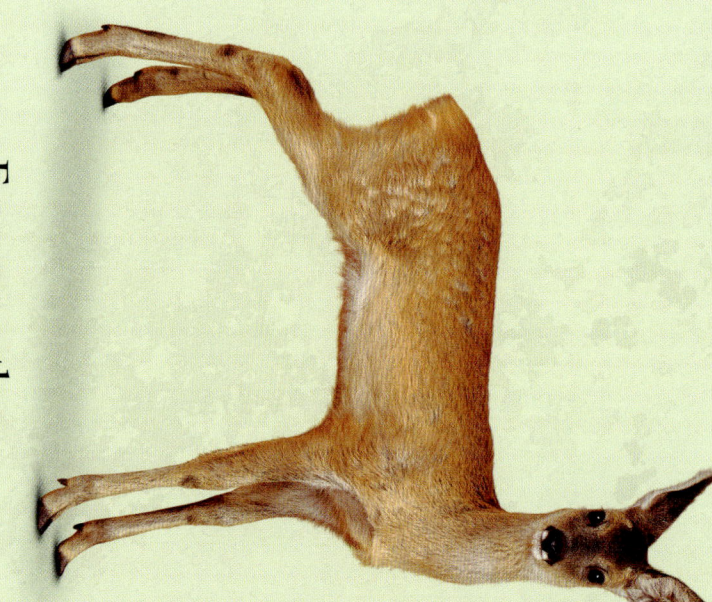

Four months

Now that I am big enough,
I can join the rest of my family.
My white spots start to fade.

My antlers begin to grow.
I can now roam the woods on my own,
and find myself a new home.

Ten months

Six months

How did they grow?

Mouse pup

Squirrel kit

Owlet

Fox cub

Fawn

DK | Penguin Random House

US Senior Editor Shannon Beatty
Project Editor Manisha Majithia
Assistant Editor Gunjan Mewati
Project Art Editors Charlotte Jennings, Kanika Kalra
Assistant Art Editor Aishwariya Chattoraj
Jacket Designer Rashika Kachroo
Jacket Coordinator Issy Walsh
DTP Designers Sachin Gupta, Syed Md Farhan
Senior Picture Researcher Vagisha Pushp
Production Editor Robert Dunn
Production Controller Magdalena Bojko
Managing Editors Jonathan Melmoth, Monica Saigal
Managing Art Editors Diane Peyton Jones,
Romi Chakraborty
Delhi Creative Heads Glenda Fernandes,
Malavika Talukder
Publishing Manager Francesca Young
Deputy Art Director Mabel Chan
Publishing Director Sarah Larter

Consultant Derek Harvey

First American Edition, 2022
Published in the United States by DK Publishing
1450 Broadway, Suite 801, New York, NY 10018

Copyright © 2022 Dorling Kindersley Limited
DK, a Division of Penguin Random House LLC
22 23 24 25 26 10 9 8 7 6 5 4 3 2 1
001-326511-Feb/2022

For the curious
www.dk.com

ACKNOWLEDGMENTS

The publisher would like to thank the following for their kind permission to reproduce their photographs:

(Key: a-above; b-below/bottom; c-center; f-far; l-left; r-right; t-top)

1 Alamy Stock Photo: F1online digitale Bildagentur GmbH / David & Micha Sheldon (bc). Dorling Kindersley: Liberty's Owl, Raptor and Reptile Centre, Hampshire, UK (bl). Dreamstime.com: Isselee (crb). 2 naturepl.com: Jose B. Ruiz (tl). 3 Alamy Stock Photo: Pally (br). Dreamstime.com: Nehru (bl). Shutterstock.com: sabyna75 (bc). 4 Alamy Stock Photo: F1online digitale Bildagentur GmbH / David & Micha Sheldon (br); Hannah Stanbury (bl). 5 Dreamstime.com: Rudmer Zwerver (tl). 6 123RF.com: sagar prajapati (ncsl). Alamy Stock Photo: imageBROKER / FLPA / David T. Grewcock (Squirrel). 7 123RF.com: bartsadowski (bc). Dreamstime.com: Eastmanphoto (br). Science Photo Library: M.H. Sharp (bl). 8 Dreamstime.com: Eastmanphoto (br). 10 Alamy Stock Photo: WILDLIFE GmbH (bc). Dorling Kindersley: Natural History Museum, London (eggs). 12 Alamy Stock Photo: WILDLIFE GmbH (bl). wonderful-Earth.net (br). 13 Dorling Kindersley: Liberty's Owl, Raptor and Reptile Centre, Hampshire, UK (tr). 18 Dreamstime.com: Isselee (l). naturepl.com: George McCarthy (b). 19 Alamy Stock Photo: R.A. Chalmers Photography (bl). Dreamstime.com: Slowmotiongli (tl). 21 Dreamstime.com: Isselee (br). 20 Alamy Stock Photo: imageBROKER / Kristin Hanisch (br). Dreamstime.com: Isselee (br); Jnrrock (bl, r). 22 Alamy Stock Photo: F1online digitale Bildagentur GmbH / David & Micha Sheldon (cr); Hannah Stanbury (cl). Dreamstime.com: Jnrrock Eastmanphoto (br); Rudmer Zwerver (fcr); Nehru (fcl). Science Photo Library: M.H. Sharp (fbl). 23 Alamy Stock Photo: imageBROKER / Kristin Hanisch (br): R.A. Chalmers Photography (tbl). WILDLIFE GmbH (tl). Dorling Kindersley: Liberty's Owl, Raptor and Reptile Centre, Hampshire, UK (fr). Dreamstime.com: Galina Drokina

Endpaper images: Front: Alamy Stock Photo: Nature Picture Library / Jane Burton tl; Dreamstime.com: Rudmer Zwerver cr, br; Spine: Dreamstime.com: Rudmer Zwerver; Background: Dreamstime.com: Galina Drokina.

Cover images: Front: Alamy Stock Photo: R.A. Chalmers Photography br; Hannah Stanbury bl; Back: Alamy Stock Photo: imageBROKER / Kristin Hanisch r; Dreamstime.com: Rudmer Zwerver bl.

All other images © Dorling Kindersley
For further information see: www.dkimages.com

FSC — MIX — Paper from responsible sources — FSC® C018179

This book was made with Forest Stewardship Council™ certified paper—one small step in DK's commitment to a sustainable future. For more information go to www.dk.com/our-green-pledge